Today is Monday.

Rory is sad.

Today is Wednesday.

Rory and mommy are in the park.

Today is Thursday.

Rory and mommy visit grandmother.

Today is Friday.

Rory plays in the kitchen.

Rory likes the big ball.

It moves!

Activities

Before You Read

1 **Read and say *Yes* or *No*.**
   a Rory is an elephant.
   b He is young.
   c He has a big tail.
   d He is happy.

After You Read

1 **Match the words and pictures.**

sister   mommy   grandmother   brother

2 **Look at the pictures. Write the correct day of the week in your notebook.**

Wednesday   Friday   Monday   Tuesday   Thursday

Pearson Education Limited
Edinburgh Gate, Harlow,
Essex CM20 2JE, England
and Associated Companies throughout the world.

ISBN: 978-1-4479-3128-7

This edition first published by Pearson Education Ltd 2014

9 10 8

Text copyright © Pearson Education Ltd 2014

The moral rights of the author have been asserted
in accordance with the Copyright Designs and Patents Act 1988

Set in 19/23pt OT Fiendstar Semibold
Printed in China
SWTC/08

Illustrations: Laura Ellen Anderson (Pickled Ink)

All rights reserved; no part of this publication may be reproduced, stored in a retrieval system, or transmitted in any form or by any means, electronic, mechanical, photocopying, recording or otherwise, without the prior written permission of the Publishers.

For a complete list of the titles available in the Pearson English Kids Readers series, please go to www.pearsonenglishkidsreaders.com. Alternatively, write to your local Pearson Education office or to Pearson English Readers Marketing Department, Pearson Education, Edinburgh Gate, Harlow, Essex CM20 2JE, England.